Peter Bell the Third

Percy Bysshe Shelley

Contents

PETER BELL THE THIRD

BY

Percy Bysshe Shelley

PETER BELL THE THIRD. BY PERCY BYSSHE SHELLEY

BY MICHING MALLECHO, ESQ.

Is it a party in a parlour,
Crammed just as they on earth were crammed,
Some sipping punch--some sipping tea;
But, as you by their faces see,
All silent, and all--damned!
"Peter Bell", by W. WORDSWORTH.

OPHELIA.--What means this, my lord?
HAMLET.--Marry, this is Miching Mallecho; it means mischief.
SHAKESPEARE.

DEDICATION.

TO THOMAS BROWN, ESQ., THE YOUNGER, H.F.

DEAR TOM--Allow me to request you to introduce Mr. Peter Bell to the
respectable family of the Fudges. Although he may fall short of those
very considerable personages in the more active properties which

characterize the Rat and the Apostate, I suspect that even you, their historian, will confess that he surpasses them in the more peculiarly legitimate qualification of intolerable dulness.

You know Mr. Examiner Hunt; well--it was he who presented me to two of the Mr. Bells. My intimacy with the younger Mr. Bell naturally sprung from this introduction to his brothers. And in presenting him to you, I have the satisfaction of being able to assure you that he is considerably the dullest of the three.

There is this particular advantage in an acquaintance with any one of the Peter Bells, that if you know one Peter Bell, you know three Peter Bells; they are not one, but three; not three, but one. An awful mystery, which, after having caused torrents of blood, and having been hymned by groans enough to deafen the music of the spheres, is at length illustrated to the satisfaction of all parties in the theological world, by the nature of Mr. Peter Bell.

Peter is a polyhedric Peter, or a Peter with many sides. He changes colours like a chameleon, and his coat like a snake. He is a Proteus of a Peter. He was at first sublime, pathetic, impressive, profound; then dull; then prosy and dull; and now dull--oh so very dull! it is an ultra-legitimate dulness.

You will perceive that it is not necessary to consider Hell and the Devil as supernatural machinery. The whole scene of my epic is in 'this world which is'--so Peter informed us before his conversion to "White Obi"--

'The world of all of us, AND WHERE
WE FIND OUR HAPPINESS, OR NOT AT ALL.'

Let me observe that I have spent six or seven days in composing this sublime piece; the orb of my moonlike genius has made the fourth part of its revolution round the dull earth which you inhabit, driving you mad, while it has retained its calmness and its splendour, and I have been fitting this its last phase 'to occupy a permanent station in the literature of my country.'

Your works, indeed, dear Tom, sell better; but mine are far superior. The public is no judge; posterity sets all to rights.

Allow me to observe that so much has been written of Peter Bell, that the present history can be considered only, like the Iliad, as a continuation of that series of cyclic poems, which have already been candidates for bestowing immortality upon, at the same time that they receive it from, his character and adventures. In this point of view I have violated no rule of syntax in beginning my composition with a conjunction; the full stop which closes the poem continued by me being, like the full stops at the end of the Iliad and Odyssey, a full stop of a very qualified import.

Hoping that the immortality which you have given to the Fudges, you will receive from them; and in the firm expectation, that when London shall be an habitation of bitterns; when St. Paul's and Westminster Abbey shall stand, shapeless and nameless ruins, in the midst of an unpeopled marsh; when the piers of Waterloo Bridge shall become the nuclei of islets of reeds and osiers, and cast the jagged shadows of their broken arches on the solitary stream, some transatlantic commentator will be weighing in the scales of some new and now unimagined system of criticism, the respective merits of the Bells and the Fudges, and their historians. I remain, dear Tom, yours sincerely,

MICHING MALLECHO.

December 1, 1819.

P.S.--Pray excuse the date of place; so soon as the profits of the
publication come in, I mean to hire lodgings in a more respectable
street.

PROLOGUE.

Peter Bells, one, two and three,
O'er the wide world wandering be.--
First, the antenatal Peter,
Wrapped in weeds of the same metre,
The so-long-predestined raiment   5
Clothed in which to walk his way meant
The second Peter; whose ambition
Is to link the proposition,
As the mean of two extremes--
(This was learned from Aldric's themes)   10
Shielding from the guilt of schism
The orthodoxal syllogism;
The First Peter--he who was
Like the shadow in the glass
Of the second, yet unripe,   15
His substantial antitype.--

Then came Peter Bell the Second,
Who henceforward must be reckoned
The body of a double soul,
And that portion of the whole   20

Without which the rest would seem
Ends of a disjointed dream.--
And the Third is he who has
O'er the grave been forced to pass
To the other side, which is,--   25
Go and try else,--just like this.

Peter Bell the First was Peter
Smugger, milder, softer, neater,
Like the soul before it is
Born from THAT world into THIS.   30
The next Peter Bell was he,
Predevote, like you and me,
To good or evil as may come;
His was the severer doom,--
For he was an evil Cotter,   35
And a polygamic Potter.
And the last is Peter Bell,
Damned since our first parents fell,
Damned eternally to Hell--
Surely he deserves it well!   40

PART 1.

DEATH.

1.
And Peter Bell, when he had been
With fresh-imported Hell-fire warmed,
Grew serious--from his dress and mien

'Twas very plainly to be seen
Peter was quite reformed.   5

2.
His eyes turned up, his mouth turned down;
His accent caught a nasal twang;
He oiled his hair; there might be heard
The grace of God in every word
Which Peter said or sang.   10

3.
But Peter now grew old, and had
An ill no doctor could unravel:
His torments almost drove him mad;--
Some said it was a fever bad--
Some swore it was the gravel.   15

4.
His holy friends then came about,
And with long preaching and persuasion
Convinced the patient that, without
The smallest shadow of a doubt,
He was predestined to damnation.   20

5.
They said--'Thy name is Peter Bell;
Thy skin is of a brimstone hue;
Alive or dead--ay, sick or well--
The one God made to rhyme with hell;
The other, I think, rhymes with you.   25

6.
Then Peter set up such a yell!--

The nurse, who with some water gruel
Was climbing up the stairs, as well
As her old legs could climb them--fell,
And broke them both--the fall was cruel.   30

7.
The Parson from the casement lept
Into the lake of Windermere--
And many an eel--though no adept
In God's right reason for it--kept
Gnawing his kidneys half a year.   35

8.
And all the rest rushed through the door
And tumbled over one another,
And broke their skulls.--Upon the floor
Meanwhile sat Peter Bell, and swore,
And cursed his father and his mother;   40

9.
And raved of God, and sin, and death,
Blaspheming like an infidel;
And said, that with his clenched teeth
He'd seize the earth from underneath,
And drag it with him down to hell.   45

10.
As he was speaking came a spasm,
And wrenched his gnashing teeth asunder;
Like one who sees a strange phantasm
He lay,--there was a silent chasm
Between his upper jaw and under.   50

11.

And yellow death lay on his face;
And a fixed smile that was not human
Told, as I understand the case,
That he was gone to the wrong place:--
I heard all this from the old woman.   55

12.

Then there came down from Langdale Pike
A cloud, with lightning, wind and hail;
It swept over the mountains like
An ocean,--and I heard it strike
The woods and crags of Grasmere vale. 60

13.

And I saw the black storm come
Nearer, minute after minute;
Its thunder made the cataracts dumb;
With hiss, and clash, and hollow hum,
It neared as if the Devil was in it.   65

14.

The Devil WAS in it:--he had bought
Peter for half-a-crown; and when
The storm which bore him vanished, nought
That in the house that storm had caught
Was ever seen again.   70

15.

The gaping neighbours came next day--
They found all vanished from the shore:
The Bible, whence he used to pray,
Half scorched under a hen-coop lay;

Smashed glass--and nothing more!　　75

PART 2.

THE DEVIL.

1.
The Devil, I safely can aver,
Has neither hoof, nor tail, nor sting;
Nor is he, as some sages swear,
A spirit, neither here nor there,
In nothing--yet in everything.　80

2.
He is--what we are; for sometimes
The Devil is a gentleman;
At others a bard bartering rhymes
For sack; a statesman spinning crimes;
A swindler, living as he can;　　85

3.
A thief, who cometh in the night,
With whole boots and net pantaloons,
Like some one whom it were not right
To mention;--or the luckless wight
From whom he steals nine silver spoons.　　90

4.
But in this case he did appear
Like a slop-merchant from Wapping,
And with smug face, and eye severe,

On every side did perk and peer
Till he saw Peter dead or napping.   95

5.
He had on an upper Benjamin
(For he was of the driving schism)
In the which he wrapped his skin
From the storm he travelled in,
For fear of rheumatism.   100

6.
He called the ghost out of the corse;--
It was exceedingly like Peter,--
Only its voice was hollow and hoarse--
It had a queerish look of course--
Its dress too was a little neater.   105

7.
The Devil knew not his name and lot;
Peter knew not that he was Bell:
Each had an upper stream of thought,
Which made all seem as it was not;
Fitting itself to all things well.   110

8.
Peter thought he had parents dear,
Brothers, sisters, cousins, cronies,
In the fens of Lincolnshire;
He perhaps had found them there
Had he gone and boldly shown his   115

9.
Solemn phiz in his own village;

Where he thought oft when a boy
He'd clomb the orchard walls to pillage
The produce of his neighbour's tillage,
With marvellous pride and joy. 120

10.
And the Devil thought he had,
'Mid the misery and confusion
Of an unjust war, just made
A fortune by the gainful trade
Of giving soldiers rations bad-- 125
The world is full of strange delusion--

11.
That he had a mansion planned
In a square like Grosvenor Square,
That he was aping fashion, and
That he now came to Westmoreland   130
To see what was romantic there.

12.
And all this, though quite ideal,--
Ready at a breath to vanish,--
Was a state not more unreal
Than the peace he could not feel,   135
Or the care he could not banish.

13.
After a little conversation,
The Devil told Peter, if he chose,
He'd bring him to the world of fashion
By giving him a situation 140
In his own service--and new clothes.

14.
And Peter bowed, quite pleased and proud,
And after waiting some few days
For a new livery--dirty yellow
Turned up with black--the wretched fellow   145
Was bowled to Hell in the Devil's chaise.

PART 3.

HELL.

1.
Hell is a city much like London--
A populous and a smoky city;
There are all sorts of people undone,
And there is little or no fun done;   150
Small justice shown, and still less pity.

2.
There is a Castles, and a Canning,
A Cobbett, and a Castlereagh;
All sorts of caitiff corpses planning
All sorts of cozening for trepanning   155
Corpses less corrupt than they.

3.
There is a ***, who has lost
His wits, or sold them, none knows which;
He walks about a double ghost,

And though as thin as Fraud almost-- 160
Ever grows more grim and rich.

4.
There is a Chancery Court; a King;
A manufacturing mob; a set
Of thieves who by themselves are sent
Similar thieves to represent; 165
An army; and a public debt.

5.
Which last is a scheme of paper money,
And means--being interpreted--
'Bees, keep your wax--give us the honey,
And we will plant, while skies are sunny, 170
Flowers, which in winter serve instead.'

6.
There is a great talk of revolution--
And a great chance of despotism--
German soldiers--camps--confusion--
Tumults--lotteries--rage--delusion-- 175
Gin--suicide--and methodism;

7.
Taxes too, on wine and bread,
And meat, and beer, and tea, and cheese,
From which those patriots pure are fed,
Who gorge before they reel to bed 180
The tenfold essence of all these.

8.
There are mincing women, mewing,

(Like cats, who amant misere,)
Of their own virtue, and pursuing
Their gentler sisters to that ruin,   185
Without which--what were chastity?

9.
Lawyers--judges--old hobnobbers
Are there--bailiffs--chancellors--
Bishops--great and little robbers--
Rhymesters--pamphleteers--stock-jobbers--   190
Men of glory in the wars,--

10.
Things whose trade is, over ladies
To lean, and flirt, and stare, and simper,
Till all that is divine in woman
Grows cruel, courteous, smooth, inhuman,   195
Crucified 'twixt a smile and whimper.

11.
Thrusting, toiling, wailing, moiling,
Frowning, preaching--such a riot!
Each with never-ceasing labour,
Whilst he thinks he cheats his neighbour,   200
Cheating his own heart of quiet.

12.
And all these meet at levees;--
Dinners convivial and political;--
Suppers of epic poets;--teas,
Where small talk dies in agonies;--   205
Breakfasts professional and critical;

13.

Lunches and snacks so aldermanic
That one would furnish forth ten dinners,
Where reigns a Cretan-tongued panic,
Lest news Russ, Dutch, or Alemannic   210
Should make some losers, and some winners--

45.

At conversazioni--balls--
Conventicles--and drawing-rooms--
Courts of law--committees--calls
Of a morning--clubs--book-stalls--   215
Churches--masquerades--and tombs.

15.

And this is Hell--and in this smother
All are damnable and damned;
Each one damning, damns the other;
They are damned by one another,   220
By none other are they damned.

16.

'Tis a lie to say, 'God damns'!
Where was Heaven's Attorney General
When they first gave out such flams?
Let there be an end of shams,   225
They are mines of poisonous mineral.

17.

Statesmen damn themselves to be
Cursed; and lawyers damn their souls
To the auction of a fee;

Churchmen damn themselves to see   230
God's sweet love in burning coals.

18.
The rich are damned, beyond all cure,
To taunt, and starve, and trample on
The weak and wretched; and the poor
Damn their broken hearts to endure   235
Stripe on stripe, with groan on groan.

19.
Sometimes the poor are damned indeed
To take,--not means for being blessed,--
But Cobbett's snuff, revenge; that weed
From which the worms that it doth feed   240
Squeeze less than they before possessed.

20.
And some few, like we know who,
Damned--but God alone knows why--
To believe their minds are given
To make this ugly Hell a Heaven;   245
In which faith they live and die.

21.
Thus, as in a town, plague-stricken,
Each man be he sound or no
Must indifferently sicken;
As when day begins to thicken, 250
None knows a pigeon from a crow,--

22.
So good and bad, sane and mad,

The oppressor and the oppressed;
Those who weep to see what others
Smile to inflict upon their brothers;   255
Lovers, haters, worst and best;

23.
All are damned--they breathe an air,
Thick, infected, joy-dispelling:
Each pursues what seems most fair,
Mining like moles, through mind, and there   260
Scoop palace-caverns vast, where Care
In throned state is ever dwelling.

PART 4.

SIN.

1.
Lo. Peter in Hell's Grosvenor Square,
A footman in the Devil's service!
And the misjudging world would swear 265
That every man in service there
To virtue would prefer vice.

2.
But Peter, though now damned, was not
What Peter was before damnation.
Men oftentimes prepare a lot   270
Which ere it finds them, is not what
Suits with their genuine station.

3.

All things that Peter saw and felt
Had a peculiar aspect to him;
And when they came within the belt   275
Of his own nature, seemed to melt,
Like cloud to cloud, into him.

4.

And so the outward world uniting
To that within him, he became
Considerably uninviting 280
To those who, meditation slighting,
Were moulded in a different frame.

5.

And he scorned them, and they scorned him;
And he scorned all they did; and they
Did all that men of their own trim   285
Are wont to do to please their whim,
Drinking, lying, swearing, play.

6.

Such were his fellow-servants; thus
His virtue, like our own, was built
Too much on that indignant fuss   290
Hypocrite Pride stirs up in us
To bully one another's guilt.

7.

He had a mind which was somehow
At once circumference and centre
Of all he might or feel or know; 295

Nothing went ever out, although
Something did ever enter.

8.
He had as much imagination
As a pint-pot;--he never could
Fancy another situation, 300
From which to dart his contemplation,
Than that wherein he stood.

9.
Yet his was individual mind,
And new created all he saw
In a new manner, and refined   305
Those new creations, and combined
Them, by a master-spirit's law.

10.
Thus--though unimaginative--
An apprehension clear, intense,
Of his mind's work, had made alive   310
The things it wrought on; I believe
Wakening a sort of thought in sense.

11.
But from the first 'twas Peter's drift
To be a kind of moral eunuch,
He touched the hem of Nature's shift,   315
Felt faint--and never dared uplift
The closest, all-concealing tunic.

12.
She laughed the while, with an arch smile,

And kissed him with a sister's kiss,
And said--My best Diogenes,   320
I love you well--but, if you please,
Tempt not again my deepest bliss.

13.
"'Tis you are cold--for I, not coy,
Yield love for love, frank, warm, and true;
And Burns, a Scottish peasant boy--   325
His errors prove it--knew my joy
More, learned friend, than you.

14.
'Boeca bacciata non perde ventura,
Anzi rinnuova come fa la luna:--
So thought Boccaccio, whose sweet words might cure a   a
Male prude, like you, from what you now endure, a
Low-tide in soul, like a stagnant laguna.

15.
Then Peter rubbed his eyes severe.
And smoothed his spacious forehead down
With his broad palm;--'twixt love and fear,   335
He looked, as he no doubt felt, queer,
And in his dream sate down.

16.
The Devil was no uncommon creature;
A leaden-witted thief--just huddled
Out of the dross and scum of nature;   340
A toad-like lump of limb and feature,
With mind, and heart, and fancy muddled.

17.

He was that heavy, dull, cold thing,
The spirit of evil well may be:
A drone too base to have a sting;   345
Who gluts, and grimes his lazy wing,
And calls lust, luxury.

18.

Now he was quite the kind of wight
Round whom collect, at a fixed aera,
Venison, turtle, hock, and claret,--   350
Good cheer--and those who come to share it--
And best East Indian madeira!

19.

It was his fancy to invite
Men of science, wit, and learning,
Who came to lend each other light;   355
He proudly thought that his gold's might
Had set those spirits burning.

20.

And men of learning, science, wit,
Considered him as you and I
Think of some rotten tree, and sit   360
Lounging and dining under it,
Exposed to the wide sky.

21.

And all the while with loose fat smile,
The willing wretch sat winking there,
Believing 'twas his power that made   365
That jovial scene--and that all paid

Homage to his unnoticed chair.

22.
Though to be sure this place was Hell;
He was the Devil--and all they--
What though the claret circled well,   370
And wit, like ocean, rose and fell?--
Were damned eternally.

PART 5.

GRACE.

1.
Among the guests who often stayed
Till the Devil's petits-soupers,
A man there came, fair as a maid,   375
And Peter noted what he said,
Standing behind his master's chair.

2.
He was a mighty poet--and
A subtle-souled psychologist;
All things he seemed to understand,   380
Of old or new--of sea or land--
But his own mind--which was a mist.

3.
This was a man who might have turned
Hell into Heaven--and so in gladness

A Heaven unto himself have earned;   385
But he in shadows undiscerned
Trusted.--and damned himself to madness.

4.
He spoke of poetry, and how
'Divine it was--a light--a love--
A spirit which like wind doth blow   390
As it listeth, to and fro;
A dew rained down from God above;

5.
'A power which comes and goes like dream,
And which none can ever trace--
Heaven's light on earth--Truth's brightest beam.'   395
And when he ceased there lay the gleam
Of those words upon his face.

6.
Now Peter, when he heard such talk,
Would, heedless of a broken pate,
Stand like a man asleep, or balk 400
Some wishing guest of knife or fork,
Or drop and break his master's plate.

7.
At night he oft would start and wake
Like a lover, and began
In a wild measure songs to make   405
On moor, and glen, and rocky lake,
And on the heart of man--

8.
And on the universal sky--
And the wide earth's bosom green,--
And the sweet, strange mystery 410
Of what beyond these things may lie,
And yet remain unseen.

9.
For in his thought he visited
The spots in which, ere dead and damned,
He his wayward life had led;   415
Yet knew not whence the thoughts were fed
Which thus his fancy crammed.

10.
And these obscure remembrances
Stirred such harmony in Peter,
That, whensoever he should please,   420
He could speak of rocks and trees
In poetic metre.

11.
For though it was without a sense
Of memory, yet he remembered well
Many a ditch and quick-set fence;   425
Of lakes he had intelligence,
He knew something of heath and fell.

12.
He had also dim recollections
Of pedlars tramping on their rounds;
Milk-pans and pails; and odd collections   430
Of saws, and proverbs; and reflections

Old parsons make in burying-grounds.

13.
But Peter's verse was clear, and came
Announcing from the frozen hearth
Of a cold age, that none might tame   435
The soul of that diviner flame
It augured to the Earth:

14.
Like gentle rains, on the dry plains,
Making that green which late was gray,
Or like the sudden moon, that stains   440
Some gloomy chamber's window-panes
With a broad light like day.

15.
For language was in Peter's hand
Like clay while he was yet a potter;
And he made songs for all the land,   445
Sweet both to feel and understand,
As pipkins late to mountain Cotter.

16.
And Mr. --, the bookseller,
Gave twenty pounds for some;--then scorning
A footman's yellow coat to wear,   450
Peter, too proud of heart, I fear,
Instantly gave the Devil warning.

17.
Whereat the Devil took offence,
And swore in his soul a great oath then,

'That for his damned impertinence   455
He'd bring him to a proper sense
Of what was due to gentlemen!'

PART 6.

DAMNATION.

1.
'O that mine enemy had written
A book!'--cried Job:--a fearful curse,
If to the Arab, as the Briton,   460
'Twas galling to be critic-bitten:--
The Devil to Peter wished no worse.

2.
When Peter's next new book found vent,
The Devil to all the first Reviews
A copy of it slyly sent,   465
With five-pound note as compliment,
And this short notice--'Pray abuse.'

3.
Then seriatim, month and quarter,
Appeared such mad tirades.--One said--
'Peter seduced Mrs. Foy's daughter,   470
Then drowned the mother in Ullswater,
The last thing as he went to bed.'

4.
Another--'Let him shave his head!

Where's Dr. Willis?--Or is he joking?
What does the rascal mean or hope,   475
No longer imitating Pope,
In that barbarian Shakespeare poking?'

5.
One more, 'Is incest not enough?
And must there be adultery too?
Grace after meat? Miscreant and Liar!   480
Thief! Blackguard! Scoundrel! Fool! hell-fire
Is twenty times too good for you.

6.
'By that last book of yours WE think
You've double damned yourself to scorn;
We warned you whilst yet on the brink   485
You stood. From your black name will shrink
The babe that is unborn.'

7.
All these Reviews the Devil made
Up in a parcel, which he had
Safely to Peter's house conveyed.   490
For carriage, tenpence Peter paid--
Untied them--read them--went half mad.

8.
'What!' cried he, 'this is my reward
For nights of thought, and days, of toil?
Do poets, but to be abhorred   495
By men of whom they never heard,
Consume their spirits' oil?

9.

'What have I done to them?--and who
IS Mrs. Foy? 'Tis very cruel
To speak of me and Betty so!   500
Adultery! God defend me! Oh!
I've half a mind to fight a duel.

10.

'Or,' cried he, a grave look collecting,
'Is it my genius, like the moon,
Sets those who stand her face inspecting,   505
That face within their brain reflecting,
Like a crazed bell-chime, out of tune?'

11.

For Peter did not know the town,
But thought, as country readers do,
For half a guinea or a crown,   510
He bought oblivion or renown
From God's own voice in a review.

12.

All Peter did on this occasion
Was, writing some sad stuff in prose.
It is a dangerous invasion   515
When poets criticize; their station
Is to delight, not pose.

13.

The Devil then sent to Leipsic fair
For Born's translation of Kant's book;
A world of words, tail foremost, where 520
Right--wrong--false--true--and foul--and fair

As in a lottery-wheel are shook.

14.
Five thousand crammed octavo pages
Of German psychologics,--he
Who his furor verborum assuages   525
Thereon, deserves just seven months' wages
More than will e'er be due to me.

15.
I looked on them nine several days,
And then I saw that they were bad;
A friend, too, spoke in their dispraise,--530
He never read them;--with amaze
I found Sir William Drummond had.

16.
When the book came, the Devil sent
It to P. Verbovale, Esquire,
With a brief note of compliment,   535
By that night's Carlisle mail. It went,
And set his soul on fire.

17.
Fire, which ex luce praebens fumum,
Made him beyond the bottom see
Of truth's clear well--when I and you, Ma'am, 540
Go, as we shall do, subter humum,
We may know more than he.

18.
Now Peter ran to seed in soul
Into a walking paradox;

For he was neither part nor whole,   545
Nor good, nor bad--nor knave nor fool;
--Among the woods and rocks

19.
Furious he rode, where late he ran,
Lashing and spurring his tame hobby;
Turned to a formal puritan,   550
A solemn and unsexual man,--
He half believed "White Obi".

20.
This steed in vision he would ride,
High trotting over nine-inch bridges,
With Flibbertigibbet, imp of pride,   555
Mocking and mowing by his side--
A mad-brained goblin for a guide--
Over corn-fields, gates, and hedges.

21.
After these ghastly rides, he came
Home to his heart, and found from thence   560
Much stolen of its accustomed flame;
His thoughts grew weak, drowsy, and lame
Of their intelligence.

22.
To Peter's view, all seemed one hue;
He was no Whig, he was no Tory;   565
No Deist and no Christian he;--
He got so subtle, that to be
Nothing, was all his glory.

23.

One single point in his belief
From his organization sprung,   570
The heart-enrooted faith, the chief
Ear in his doctrines' blighted sheaf,
That 'Happiness is wrong';

24.

So thought Calvin and Dominic;
So think their fierce successors, who   575
Even now would neither stint nor stick
Our flesh from off our bones to pick,
If they might 'do their do.'

25.

His morals thus were undermined:--
The old Peter--the hard, old Potter--   580
Was born anew within his mind;
He grew dull, harsh, sly, unrefined,
As when he tramped beside the Otter.

26.

In the death hues of agony
Lambently flashing from a fish,   585
Now Peter felt amused to see
Shades like a rainbow's rise and flee,
Mixed with a certain hungry wish.

27.

So in his Country's dying face
He looked--and, lovely as she lay,   590
Seeking in vain his last embrace,
Wailing her own abandoned case,

With hardened sneer he turned away:

28.
And coolly to his own soul said;--
'Do you not think that we might make 595
A poem on her when she's dead:--
Or, no--a thought is in my head--
Her shroud for a new sheet I'll take:

29.
'My wife wants one.--Let who will bury
This mangled corpse! And I and you,   600
My dearest Soul, will then make merry,
As the Prince Regent did with Sherry,--'
'Ay--and at last desert me too.'

30.
And so his Soul would not be gay,
But moaned within him; like a fawn   605
Moaning within a cave, it lay
Wounded and wasting, day by day,
Till all its life of life was gone.

31.
As troubled skies stain waters clear,
The storm in Peter's heart and mind   610
Now made his verses dark and queer:
They were the ghosts of what they were,
Shaking dim grave-clothes in the wind.

32.
For he now raved enormous folly,
Of Baptisms, Sunday-schools, and Graves,   615

'Twould make George Colman melancholy
To have heard him, like a male Molly,
Chanting those stupid staves.

33.
Yet the Reviews, who heaped abuse
On Peter while he wrote for freedom,   620
So soon as in his song they spy
The folly which soothes tyranny,
Praise him, for those who feed 'em.

34.
'He was a man, too great to scan;--
A planet lost in truth's keen rays:--   625
His virtue, awful and prodigious;--
He was the most sublime, religious,
Pure-minded Poet of these days.'

35.
As soon as he read that, cried Peter,
'Eureka! I have found the way   630
To make a better thing of metre
Than e'er was made by living creature
Up to this blessed day.'

36.
Then Peter wrote odes to the Devil;--
In one of which he meekly said: 635
'May Carnage and Slaughter,
Thy niece and thy daughter,
May Rapine and Famine,
Thy gorge ever cramming,
Glut thee with living and dead!   640

37.
'May Death and Damnation,
And Consternation,
Flit up from Hell with pure intent!
Slash them at Manchester,
Glasgow, Leeds, and Chester;   645
Drench all with blood from Avon to Trent.

38.
'Let thy body-guard yeomen
Hew down babes and women,
And laugh with bold triumph till Heaven be rent!
When Moloch in Jewry   650
Munched children with fury,
It was thou, Devil, dining with pure intent.

PART 7.

DOUBLE DAMNATION.

1.
The Devil now knew his proper cue.--
Soon as he read the ode, he drove
To his friend Lord MacMurderchouse's,655
A man of interest in both houses,
And said:--'For money or for love,

2.
'Pray find some cure or sinecure;
To feed from the superfluous taxes

A friend of ours--a poet--fewer 660
Have fluttered tamer to the lure
Than he.' His lordship stands and racks his

3.
Stupid brains, while one might count
As many beads as he had boroughs,--
At length replies; from his mean front, 665
Like one who rubs out an account,
Smoothing away the unmeaning furrows:

4.
'It happens fortunately, dear Sir,
I can. I hope I need require
No pledge from you, that he will stir   670
In our affairs;--like Oliver.
That he'll be worthy of his hire.'

5.
These words exchanged, the news sent off
To Peter, home the Devil hied,--
Took to his bed; he had no cough,   675
No doctor,--meat and drink enough.--
Yet that same night he died.

6.
The Devil's corpse was leaded down;
His decent heirs enjoyed his pelf,
Mourning-coaches, many a one, 680
Followed his hearse along the town:--
Where was the Devil himself?

7.

When Peter heard of his promotion,
His eyes grew like two stars for bliss:
There was a bow of sleek devotion   685
Engendering in his back; each motion
Seemed a Lord's shoe to kiss.

8.

He hired a house, bought plate, and made
A genteel drive up to his door,
With sifted gravel neatly laid,-- 690
As if defying all who said,
Peter was ever poor.

9.

But a disease soon struck into
The very life and soul of Peter--
He walked about--slept--had the hue   695
Of health upon his cheeks--and few
Dug better--none a heartier eater.

10.

And yet a strange and horrid curse
Clung upon Peter, night and day;
Month after month the thing grew worse,   700
And deadlier than in this my verse
I can find strength to say.

11.

Peter was dull--he was at first
Dull--oh, so dull--so very dull!
Whether he talked, wrote, or rehearsed--   705
Still with this dulness was he cursed--

Dull--beyond all conception--dull.

12.
No one could read his books--no mortal,
But a few natural friends, would hear him;
The parson came not near his portal;   710
His state was like that of the immortal
Described by Swift--no man could bear him.

13.
His sister, wife, and children yawned,
With a long, slow, and drear ennui,
All human patience far beyond; 715
Their hopes of Heaven each would have pawned,
Anywhere else to be.

14.
But in his verse, and in his prose,
The essence of his dulness was
Concentred and compressed so close,   720
'Twould have made Guatimozin doze
On his red gridiron of brass.

15.
A printer's boy, folding those pages,
Fell slumbrously upon one side;
Like those famed Seven who slept three ages.   725
To wakeful frenzy's vigil--rages,
As opiates, were the same applied.

16.
Even the Reviewers who were hired
To do the work of his reviewing,

With adamantine nerves, grew tired;-- 730
Gaping and torpid they retired,
To dream of what they should be doing.

17.
And worse and worse, the drowsy curse
Yawned in him, till it grew a pest--
A wide contagious atmosphere, 735
Creeping like cold through all things near;
A power to infect and to infest.

18.
His servant-maids and dogs grew dull;
His kitten, late a sportive elf;
The woods and lakes, so beautiful,   740
Of dim stupidity were full.
All grew dull as Peter's self.

19.
The earth under his feet--the springs,
Which lived within it a quick life,
The air, the winds of many wings,   745
That fan it with new murmurings,
Were dead to their harmonious strife.

20.
The birds and beasts within the wood,
The insects, and each creeping thing,
Were now a silent multitude;   750
Love's work was left unwrought--no brood
Near Peter's house took wing.

21.

And every neighbouring cottager
Stupidly yawned upon the other:
No jackass brayed; no little cur   755
Cocked up his ears;--no man would stir
To save a dying mother.

22.
Yet all from that charmed district went
But some half-idiot and half-knave,
Who rather than pay any rent,   760
Would live with marvellous content,
Over his father's grave.

23.
No bailiff dared within that space,
For fear of the dull charm, to enter;
A man would bear upon his face,   765
For fifteen months in any case,
The yawn of such a venture.

24.
Seven miles above--below--around--
This pest of dulness holds its sway;
A ghastly life without a sound;   770
To Peter's soul the spell is bound--
How should it ever pass away?

The Codes Of Hammurabi And Moses
W. W. Davies

QTY

The discovery of the Hammurabi Code is one of the greatest achievements of archaeology, and is of paramount interest, not only to the student of the Bible, but also to all those interested in ancient history...

Religion   **ISBN: *1-59462-338-4***   **Pages:132**

MSRP $12.95

The Theory of Moral Sentiments
Adam Smith

QTY

This work from 1749. contains original theories of conscience amd moral judgment and it is the foundation for systemof morals.

Philosophy   **ISBN: *1-59462-777-0***   **Pages:536**

MSRP $19.95

Jessica's First Prayer
Hesba Stretton

QTY

In a screened and secluded corner of one of the many railway-bridges which span the streets of London there could be seen a few years ago, from five o'clock every morning until half past eight, a tidily set-out coffee-stall, consisting of a trestle and board, upon which stood two large tin cans, with a small fire of charcoal burning under each so as to keep the coffee boiling during the early hours of the morning when the work-people were thronging into the city on their way to their daily toil...

Pages:84

Childrens   **ISBN: *1-59462-373-2***   *MSRP $9.95*

My Life and Work
Henry Ford

QTY

Henry Ford revolutionized the world with his implementation of mass production for the Model T automobile. Gain valuable business insight into his life and work with his own auto-biography... "We have only started on our development of our country we have not as yet, with all our talk of wonderful progress, done more than scratch the surface. The progress has been wonderful enough but..."

Pages:300

Biographies/   **ISBN: *1-59462-198-5***   *MSRP $21.95*

The Art of Cross-Examination
Francis Wellman

QTY

I presume it is the experience of every author, after his first book is published upon an important subject, to be almost overwhelmed with a wealth of ideas and illustrations which could readily have been included in his book, and which to his own mind, at least, seem to make a second edition inevitable. Such certainly was the case with me; and when the first edition had reached its sixth impression in five months, I rejoiced to learn that it seemed to my publishers that the book had met with a sufficiently favorable reception to justify a second and considerably enlarged edition. ..

Pages:412

Reference   **ISBN:** *1-59462-647-2*   *MSRP $19.95*

On the Duty of Civil Disobedience
Henry David Thoreau

QTY

Thoreau wrote his famous essay, On the Duty of Civil Disobedience, as a protest against an unjust but popular war and the immoral but popular institution of slave-owning. He did more than write—he declined to pay his taxes, and was hauled off to gaol in consequence. Who can say how much this refusal of his hastened the end of the war and of slavery ?

Law   **ISBN:** *1-59462-747-9*   **Pages:48**
MSRP $7.45

Dream Psychology Psychoanalysis for Beginners
Sigmund Freud

QTY

Sigmund Freud, born Sigismund Schlomo Freud (May 6, 1856 - September 23, 1939), was a Jewish-Austrian neurologist and psychiatrist who co-founded the psychoanalytic school of psychology. Freud is best known for his theories of the unconscious mind, especially involving the mechanism of repression; his redefinition of sexual desire as mobile and directed towards a wide variety of objects; and his therapeutic techniques, especially his understanding of transference in the therapeutic relationship and the presumed value of dreams as sources of insight into unconscious desires.

Pages:196

Psychology   **ISBN:** *1-59462-905-6*   *MSRP $15.45*

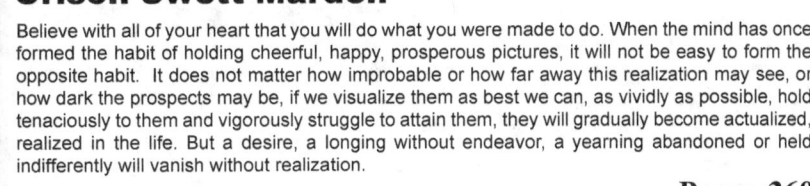

The Miracle of Right Thought
Orison Swett Marden

QTY

Believe with all of your heart that you will do what you were made to do. When the mind has once formed the habit of holding cheerful, happy, prosperous pictures, it will not be easy to form the opposite habit. It does not matter how improbable or how far away this realization may see, or how dark the prospects may be, if we visualize them as best we can, as vividly as possible, hold tenaciously to them and vigorously struggle to attain them, they will gradually become actualized, realized in the life. But a desire, a longing without endeavor, a yearning abandoned or held indifferently will vanish without realization.

Pages:360

Self Help   **ISBN:** *1-59462-644-8*   *MSRP $25.45*

QTY

The Rosicrucian Cosmo-Conception Mystic Christianity by *Max Heindel*   ISBN: *1-59462-188-8*   **$38.95**
The Rosicrucian Cosmo-conception is not dogmatic, neither does it appeal to any other authority than the reason of the student. It is: not controversial, but is: sent forth in the, hope that it may help to clear...   New Age/Religion Pages 646

Abandonment To Divine Providence by *Jean-Pierre de Caussade*   ISBN: *1-59462-228-0*   **$25.95**
"The Rev. Jean Pierre de Caussade was one of the most remarkable spiritual writers of the Society of Jesus in France in the 18th Century. His death took place at Toulouse in 1751. His works have gone through many editions and have been republished...   Inspirational/Religion Pages 400

Mental Chemistry by *Charles Haanel*   ISBN: *1-59462-192-6*   **$23.95**
Mental Chemistry allows the change of material conditions by combining and appropriately utilizing the power of the mind. Much like applied chemistry creates something new and unique out of careful combinations of chemicals the mastery of mental chemistry...   New Age Pages 354

The Letters of Robert Browning and Elizabeth Barret Barrett 1845-1846 vol II   ISBN: *1-59462-193-4*   **$35.95**
by *Robert Browning* and *Elizabeth Barrett*   Biographies Pages 596

Gleanings In Genesis (volume I) by *Arthur W. Pink*   ISBN: *1-59462-130-6*   **$27.45**
Appropriately has Genesis been termed "the seed plot of the Bible" for in it we have, in germ form, almost all of the great doctrines which are afterwards fully developed in the books of Scripture which follow...   Religion/Inspirational Pages 420

The Master Key by *L. W. de Laurence*   ISBN: *1-59462-001-6*   **$30.95**
In no branch of human knowledge has there been a more lively increase of the spirit of research during the past few years than in the study of Psychology, Concentration and Mental Discipline. The requests for authentic lessons in Thought Control, Mental Discipline and...   New Age/Business Pages 422

The Lesser Key Of Solomon Goetia by *L. W. de Laurence*   ISBN: *1-59462-092-X*   **$9.95**
This translation of the first book of the "Lernegton" which is now for the first time made accessible to students of Talismanic Magic was done, after careful collation and edition, from numerous Ancient Manuscripts in Hebrew, Latin, and French...   New Age/Occult Pages 92

Rubaiyat Of Omar Khayyam by *Edward Fitzgerald*   ISBN:*1-59462-332-5*   **$13.95**
Edward Fitzgerald, whom the world has already learned, in spite of his own efforts to remain within the shadow of anonymity, to look upon as one of the rarest poets of the century, was born at Bredfield, in Suffolk, on the 31st of March, 1809. He was the third son of John Purcell...   Music Pages 172

Ancient Law by *Henry Maine*   ISBN: *1-59462-128-4*   **$29.95**
The chief object of the following pages is to indicate some of the earliest ideas of mankind, as they are reflected in Ancient Law, and to point out the relation of those ideas to modern thought.   Religion/History Pages 452

Far-Away Stories by *William J. Locke*   ISBN: *1-59462-129-2*   **$19.45**
"Good wine needs no bush, but a collection of mixed vintages does. And this book is just such a collection. Some of the stories I do not want to remain buried for ever in the museum files of dead magazine-numbers an author's not unpardonable vanity..."   Fiction Pages 272

Life of David Crockett by *David Crockett*   ISBN: *1-59462-250-7*   **$27.45**
"Colonel David Crockett was one of the most remarkable men of the times in which he lived. Born in humble life, but gifted with a strong will, an indomitable courage, and unremitting perseverance...   Biographies/New Age Pages 424

Lip-Reading by *Edward Nitchie*   ISBN: *1-59462-206-X*   **$25.95**
Edward B. Nitchie, founder of the New York School for the Hard of Hearing, now the Nitchie School of Lip-Reading, Inc, wrote "LIP-READING Principles and Practice". The development and perfecting of this meritorious work on lip-reading was an undertaking...   How-to Pages 400

A Handbook of Suggestive Therapeutics, Applied Hypnotism, Psychic Science   ISBN: *1-59462-214-0*   **$24.95**
by *Henry Munro*   Health/New Age/Health/Self-help Pages 376

A Doll's House: and Two Other Plays by *Henrik Ibsen*   ISBN: *1-59462-112-8*   **$19.95**
Henrik Ibsen created this classic when in revolutionary 1848 Rome. Introducing some striking concepts in playwriting for the realist genre, this play has been studied the world over.   Fiction/Classics/Plays 308

The Light of Asia by *sir Edwin Arnold*   ISBN: *1-59462-204-5*   **$13.95**
In this poetic masterpiece, Edwin Arnold describes the life and teachings of Buddha. The man who was to become known as Buddha to the world was born as Prince Gautama of India but he rejected the worldly riches and abandoned the reigns of power when...   Religion/History/Biographies Pages 170

The Complete Works of Guy de Maupassant by *Guy de Maupassant*   ISBN: *1-59462-157-8*   **$16.95**
"For days and days, nights and nights, I had dreamed of that first kiss which was to consecrate our engagement, and I knew not on what spot I should put my lips..."   Fiction/Classics Pages 240

The Art of Cross-Examination by *Francis L. Wellman*   ISBN: *1-59462-309-0*   **$26.95**
Written by a renowned trial lawyer, Wellman imparts his experience and uses case studies to explain how to use psychology to extract desired information through questioning.   How-to/Science/Reference Pages 408

Answered or Unanswered? by *Louisa Vaughan*   ISBN: *1-59462-248-5*   **$10.95**
Miracles of Faith in China   Religion Pages 112

The Edinburgh Lectures on Mental Science (1909) by *Thomas*   ISBN: *1-59462-008-3*   **$11.95**
This book contains the substance of a course of lectures recently given by the writer in the Queen Street Hail, Edinburgh. Its purpose is to indicate the Natural Principles governing the relation between Mental Action and Material Conditions...   New Age/Psychology Pages 148

Ayesha by *H. Rider Haggard*   ISBN: *1-59462-301-5*   **$24.95**
Verily and indeed it is the unexpected that happens! Probably if there was one person upon the earth from whom the Editor of this, and of a certain previous history, did not expect to hear again...   Classics Pages 380

Ayala's Angel by *Anthony Trollope*   ISBN: *1-59462-352-X*   **$29.95**
The two girls were both pretty, but Lucy who was twenty-one who supposed to be simple and comparatively unattractive, whereas Ayala was credited, as her Bombwhat romantic name might show, with poetic charm and a taste for romance. Ayala when her father died was nineteen...   Fiction Pages 484

The American Commonwealth by *James Bryce*   ISBN: *1-59462-286-8*   **$34.45**
An interpretation of American democratic political theory. It examines political mechanics and society from the perspective of Scotsman James Bryce   Politics Pages 572

Stories of the Pilgrims by *Margaret P. Pumphrey*   ISBN: *1-59462-116-0*   **$17.95**
This book explores pilgrims religious oppression in England as well as their escape to Holland and eventual crossing to America on the Mayflower, and their early days in New England...   History Pages 268

www.bookjungle.com *email: sales@bookjungle.com fax: 630-214-0564 mail: Book Jungle PO Box 2226 Champaign, IL 61825*

QTY

The Fasting Cure by *Sinclair Upton*   ISBN: *1-59462-222-1* $13.95
In the Cosmopolitan Magazine for May, 1910, and in the Contemporary Review (London) for April, 1910, I published an article dealing with my experiences in fasting. I have written a great many magazine articles, but never one which attracted so much attention... New Age/Self Help/Health Pages 164

Hebrew Astrology by *Sepharial*   ISBN: *1-59462-308-2* $13.45
In these days of advanced thinking it is a matter of common observation that we have left many of the old landmarks behind and that we are now pressing forward to greater heights and to a wider horizon than that which represented the mind-content of our progenitors...   Astrology Pages 144

Thought Vibration or The Law of Attraction in the Thought World   ISBN: *1-59462-127-6* $12.95

by *William Walker Atkinson*   *Psychology/Religion Pages 144*

Optimism by *Helen Keller*   ISBN: *1-59462-108-X* $15.95
Helen Keller was blind, deaf, and mute since 19 months old, yet famously learned how to overcome these handicaps, communicate with the world, and spread her lectures promoting optimism. An inspiring read for everyone...   Biographies/Inspirational Pages 84

Sara Crewe by *Frances Burnett*   ISBN: *1-59462-360-0* $9.45
In the first place, Miss Minchin lived in London. Her home was a large, dull, tall one, in a large, dull square, where all the houses were alike, and all the sparrows were alike, and where all the door-knockers made the same heavy sound...   Childrens/Classic Pages 88

The Autobiography of Benjamin Franklin by *Benjamin Franklin*   ISBN: *1-59462-135-7* $24.95
The Autobiography of Benjamin Franklin has probably been more extensively read than any other American historical work, and no other book of its kind has had such ups and downs of fortune. Franklin lived for many years in England, where he was agent...   Biographies/History Pages 332

Name	
Email	
Telephone	
Address	
City, State ZIP	

☐ **Credit Card**   ☐ **Check / Money Order**

Credit Card Number	
Expiration Date	
Signature	

Please Mail to: Book Jungle
                                 PO Box 2226
                                 Champaign, IL 61825
or Fax to: *630-214-0564*

ORDERING INFORMATION

web: *www.bookjungle.com*
email: *sales@bookjungle.com*
fax: *630-214-0564*
mail: *Book Jungle PO Box 2226 Champaign, IL 61825*
or PayPal *to sales@bookjungle.com*

Please contact us for bulk discounts

DIRECT-ORDER TERMS

**20% Discount if You Order
Two or More Books**
Free Domestic Shipping!
Accepted: Master Card, Visa,
Discover, American Express